Printed in the United States of America

First Edition

10 9 8 7 6 5 4 3 2 1

Library of Congress Catalog Card Number: 2004112386

ISBN 0-7868-3520-6

Visit www.disneybooks.com

MY SIDE
of the Story

By Lucky

As told to Daphne Skinner

Illustrated by the Disney Storybook Artists

Disney PRESS

New York

Runt of the Litter

My name is Lucky, and here's why. When I was born I was so small and weak that everybody thought I was dead! My mother says that if it hadn't been for our pet Roger, who rubbed me with a towel until I wiggled, she would only have fourteen beautiful spotted children today instead of fifteen. How lucky was that? And then, when my spots came in and formed a cool horseshoe shape on my back, it sealed the deal—Lucky I was.

I like that story.

Whenever my mother tells it I get a big, warm feeling about Roger that makes my tail wag very hard. Roger is a fine pet, and so is his mate, Anita. They are friendly, alert, and easy to train. My mother—whose name is Perdita, but who's called Perdy—knows lots of stories about them. So does my father, Pongo.

There's one about how Roger and Anita met in the park and fell in love because Dad planned it. (He thought Mom was really cute.) And there's another about the day both couples got married. And there's the one about the extra bones they gave Mom before she had us, so we'd all be strong, healthy Dalmatians.

"We're lucky to have Roger and Anita, and not just because they're obedient," says Mom. We know what she means. When we were tiny pups we met a human who was so bad that nobody would *ever* want her for a pet.

Her name was Cruella De Vil.

I don't remember the first time Cruella came to our house, because I was too little—only a few days old. My fourteen brothers and sisters and I were all fast asleep when she stormed in.

Mom and Dad remember, though. They've told us the story many times. "She was wearing a big fur coat, and her bark was loud and raspy," says Dad. "She wanted to buy you pups, and she demanded to see all of you right away, even though Anita told her you were sleeping. She kept insisting until Anita showed her Lucky."

"But he's just a little white lump!" cried Cruella, curling her lip in disgust. "Are they all like that?"

Anita said yes.

"Never mind, then," Cruella snapped. "I want spotted puppies, not white ones. These are mongrels!"

And that, says Dad, is when Nanny got angry.

Nanny lives with us. She cleans the house and feeds all of us and she scratches our bellies at least once a day, so we like her a lot.

"They're not mongrels!" she objected. "They're fine Dalmatian puppies, and they'll be getting their spots soon enough!"

That made Cruella change her mind. "In that case," she announced, "I'll take them. Wrap them up."

"But of course Roger wouldn't allow that," says my dad. "He was even angrier than Nanny, and he told Cruella very firmly that you puppies weren't for sale. At first she didn't believe him. But when she realized he meant business, she got angry. Very angry."

"So angry that she did terrible things," I always add at this point. And then, if I'm *really* lucky, Mom and Dad let me tell the rest of the story. Which is what I'm going to do now.

2

The Bad Men

In the weeks after Cruella's visit, all we puppies did was eat and sleep and have accidents on the rug. That wasn't really exciting, except maybe to Nanny, who had to clean up after us. She soon taught us the difference between inside the house, where it was not okay to have accidents, and outside the house, where it was. After we learned that, we grew some more. We also played, and snuggled with Mom and Dad, and got belly rubs, and watched TV. Life was good.

And then the Good-for-Nothing Hoodlums came.

That's what Nanny called them, anyway. They came to the house one night while Mom and Dad were out walking Roger and Anita. Nanny tried to stop them, but they forced their way in and locked her in the attic. "Good-for-Nothing Hoodlums!" Nanny shouted, over and over again. "Let me out!"

But they didn't. Their names changed, though. When they stuffed us all into a big bag and locked us in their truck, Nanny called them Filthy Rotten Scoundrels. She sounded like she may have been crying.

In the truck we heard them calling each other Jasper and Horace, but we named them the Bad Men because they did so many bad things. They upset Nanny and stole us from our pets *and* our parents, and they wouldn't pay attention to us when we asked to be taken back home, even though we were very polite and didn't bark too loudly.

After they ignored us for a long time, we stopped asking. My brother Patch tried to scratch and chew his way out of the bag and so did I, but we couldn't. So we huddled together for comfort.

Then Patch said, "They're taking us far away from home." Patch is clever, and often right.

"I'm so hungry!" said Rolly, who is always hungry.

"I'm scared," whimpered Penny, who is hardly ever afraid.

Me too, I thought. I kept wondering why the Bad Men had stolen us and where we were going. What would happen when the trip was over? Would they feed us? Or walk us? Or let us watch TV? Somehow I knew they wouldn't be rubbing our bellies, and for a moment, I felt very whiny, missing everything and everybody from home. But I'm not the runt of the litter anymore, so I didn't whine, though it was hard not to.

Finally the truck stopped and the Bad Men hauled us out, grunting and complaining about how heavy we were. We heard loud squeaks ("Doors," said Patch) and quiet squeaks ("Mice," said Penny), but we couldn't see where we were until the Bad Men dropped the bag and opened it.

3

Tibs

When we tumbled out, we were in a dark, chilly house with dusty floors and cobwebby furniture. But the amazing thing was that the house was full of puppies, and they were all Dalmatians, just like us! There were so many we couldn't count them—even Patch gave up. Of course we were glad to see each other, and spent a long time wagging our tails and sniffing. Once we were acquainted, we learned that the puppies came from pet shops all over London. There were eighty-four of them.

"But why?" I asked.

"We don't know," said one of them. "The humans just tell us to shut up when we ask."

"They're mean," said another puppy. "I want to bite them on their noses."

"They hardly feed us, either," said a third.

"Oh, no!" yipped Rolly. "I'm so hungry!"

I was wishing for a snack, too, but it didn't look as if the Bad Men were going to feed us. They had settled down to watch TV. When humans do that, first they forget about everything else, and then they fall asleep.

"Let's go exploring," I said. "Maybe we'll find some food." That was all Rolly had to hear. Soon, he and Patch and I were sniffing around the room, under the furniture and in the dusty corners.

We didn't find any food. But we did find a cat.

Actually, he found us. He appeared out of a dark corner very suddenly, and one of my brothers—I won't say who—yipped very loudly in fright.

"My name is Tibs," hissed the cat, waving his crooked orange tail. "You must be the stolen puppies."

"We are," I said. "How did you find us?"

"It was the Twilight Bark," said Tibs, describing how our parents barked out a message that we were missing the night the Bad Men stole us. "It came through loud and clear," he said. "First the dogs in your parents' neighborhood heard it. They passed it along, and by moonrise it had come out here to Suffolk. Not bad," he added, "considering how far we are from London."

"I knew it." Patch sighed.

"Don't worry," said Tibs. "We'll get you back there—" He stopped, and we all heard the deep growl of a car engine. It died suddenly, a door slammed, and the big front door of the house opened with a rusty squeal.

Tibs hid under a chair.

A tall, thin woman wrapped in furs threw the front door open.

"You imbeciles! I'm not paying you to loaf in front of a television!" she shouted. Horace and Jasper looked as if they'd been caught playing Pull the Toilet Paper, and began to stammer excuses, which she ignored. "Turn it off!" she snarled. "There's work to do!"

"Yes, Miss De Vil," said Jasper, obeying her instantly.

Cringing, we drew together into a tight puppy ball.

It was Cruella De Vil.

But I bet I didn't need to tell you that!

4

Cruella's Command

Cruella started shouting at the Bad Men in her raspy voice. "Kill them! Do it tonight!"

Sometimes my brothers and sisters and I all think the same thing, like Time to wee, or Let's chew the furniture. Now, hearing Cruella, we all thought, She means us! and we trembled.

"How . . . how do you want us to do it, miss?" asked Horace, shrinking away from her.

"I don't care!" she screeched. "Just get it done! I need their coats right away, do you understand?"

"Yes, Miss De Vil," they said meekly. But after she'd stormed out, and the growl of her car had faded away, Jasper turned the TV back on. "We'll just watch this program first," he said, settling back into his chair.

"Right," agreed Horace.

Tibs's yellow eyes gleamed. "Good," he whispered.

Good? We stared at him.

"We've got to get out of here fast, and we can do it while they're watching TV," he explained. "If we hurry, they may not notice. So," he said, "line up and climb through that hole." He pointed across the room, to a jagged opening in the wall. "Do it one by one, as quietly as you can, and wait for me at the front door."

I'll admit that I was worried about getting past the Bad Men and squeezing through the hole, but that turned out to be easy.

The hard part was waiting for the others.

I stood at the door with Patch and Penny and Rolly, watching the pups come through, counting as the group got bigger and bigger. Everybody was so quiet that we could hear the drone of the TV.

"As long as the TV is on, we'll be okay," said Penny.

"Maybe they'll fall asleep," said Patch hopefully. I'd been thinking that, too.

"Cross your paws," said Rolly.

We were up to seventy-five puppies when the TV switched off.

"Uh-oh," said Penny.

We heard the Bad Men shout, sounding very angry, and then Tibs came hurtling through the hole in the wall, crying, "Run upstairs, pups! Follow me!" so that's what we did. But we forgot about being quiet, and there was a lot of yipping and panting as we ran after Tibs, which is probably why Jasper found us so easily, even in the dark.

At first he used a friendly voice, but we all knew he was a Bad Man, and sure enough, a moment later he swung at us with a big stick. He didn't hit us, though, because Tibs leaped at him. Jasper was so startled he fell backward. We ran over him and out the door.

Then things got even more exciting.

5

Mom and Dad

We were at the front door, wondering how to get outside, when a big shaggy dog appeared at the window, barking for Tibs. The dog was called the Colonel, and he lived with Tibs and a horse called the Captain, but we didn't know that then. All we knew was that Horace tried to scare the Colonel away by throwing a chair at him, which broke the window and gave us a way out.

But before we could escape, Jasper showed up—with Tibs still hanging from his shirt by his claws. "Corner 'em!" Jasper shouted to Horace. "Corner the little mongrels, and we'll do 'em in!"

Tibs hissed and clawed until Jasper managed to fling him across the room, and soon Horace had all ninety-nine of us backed up against a wall. A couple of puppies, like me, growled fiercely at the Bad Men.

Just as Jasper raised his stick to hit us, two snarling black-and-white blurs flew through the window. One hit Jasper; the other hit Horace. This was very good to see and there was a lot of shouting and barking and scuffling as the Bad Men tried to get away. But the best thing about it was that the black-and-white blurs were our mom and dad! Our very own parents! They had found us!

It was thrilling. They were so ferocious that they scared the pants off the Bad Men. Dad bit Jasper's bottom, and Mom knocked Horace right into the fireplace! We cheered and cheered.

"Come on, everybody!" I yipped, and soon all ninety-nine of us were outside, following Tibs and the Colonel through the snow.

We had all just piled into their barn when the Captain whinnied softly. He was standing guard at a stall window. An instant later, our parents bounded into the barn.

We were so happy they were safe! Some of my brothers and sisters—I won't say who—made the Wee Wee of Joy without going outside. Nanny would have scolded them, but my parents didn't care. They were much too busy telling us how much they'd missed us, and we were too busy licking them and climbing on them.

After we'd calmed down, my parents noticed the other eighty-four puppies. They knew that Cruella had stolen us—they had learned this through the Twilight Bark—but they didn't know about the others.

"Why on earth would she want so many?" wondered my mother.

"She wants to make coats out of us," said Rolly.

My mother was so shocked that her ears stood straight up. "That woman is a devil!" she cried.

"We have to get back to London somehow," said my father.

"But what about the other pups?" asked Patch. "What'll they do?"

It hardly took a moment for my parents to decide. "We'll take them with us," said my father, and my mother thumped her tail in agreement. "Our pets would never turn them out," she said.

For a moment the barn rang with yips of relief.

Our parents thanked the Captain, the Colonel, and Tibs, and they promised to keep in contact using the Twilight Bark.

"We'll report in frequently," said the Colonel. "Never fear."

Then they wished us luck, and we set off for London.

6

Queenie, Duchess, and Princess

The countryside was covered in ice and snow, and the air was very cold. It got colder as night fell, and the wind picked up.

"This is no walk in the park, Perdy," my father said, looking grim.

"I know, Pongo," she replied. "But at least that Devil Woman hasn't found us yet. And the Colonel's news was good."

The Colonel had used the Twilight Bark to report that he, Tibs, and the Captain had stopped the Bad Men shortly after we left. "The Captain kicked them through the barn wall!" were his words.

As good as the news was, it couldn't stop the ice from stinging our paws—we were traveling on a frozen river so we wouldn't leave tracks in the snow—or the wind from biting our ears. It didn't do much for the growling in our bellies, either. Some of us whimpered a little, until our parents told us to stop because the Bad Men might hear us.

We trudged along quietly, but they found us anyway.

"Quick! Under the bridge!" whispered my father as soon as we heard their truck. We huddled together just out of sight.

Jasper said something about not seeing any tracks, and Horace said maybe we'd traveled on the ice so we wouldn't leave tracks.

"Dogs ain't that smart!" Jasper snarled, and they drove away.

"They don't know much about dogs, do they, Dad?" asked Patch.

"No, son, they don't," said my father.

"They're dumber than two rocks in a bucket," said my mother. "It's Cruella we've got to worry about."

"Right you are, as usual, Perdy," Dad said as we set off again.

The next part of the trip was the hardest yet. The snowstorm turned into a blizzard, pelting us with sleet that felt like sharp little stones. I tried to keep up, but I couldn't—I was too cold and tired.

When my father found me, I was hunched over against the wind, feeling half frozen and completely hopeless.

"Lucky! What's the matter, son?" he asked.

"My nose is frozen, and my ears are frozen, and my toes are frozen," I whimpered.

"Poor boy," he said. Then he picked me up and carried me the way my mother did when I was the runt of the litter.

"Thank you, Dad," I whispered. Just as my eyes closed, I remember thinking I was lucky to have him as my dad.

When I woke up I smelled straw, and I felt wonderfully warm—until a chilly wet nose poked me in the belly. "Get up, Lucky!" yipped Patch.

I sat up. Patch had milk on his jowls. "Where are we?" I asked.

"We're in a dairy barn," he said. "The collie over there rescued us." He pointed to a dog who was talking with my parents in a corner. "And the cows are feeding us. Their names are Queenie, Duchess, and Princess." The large creatures looked down at us from their stalls.

Queenie smiled at me. "Look at the little darling," she lowed.

"They've got lots of milk," said Patch, "and they're sharing!"

My stomach growled like an angry bulldog. I was very hungry.

"What are you waiting for?" said Patch. "Go get some."

For once I didn't argue with him.

7

Patch and Me

We had a wonderful time in the barn. We drank lots of milk and went to sleep in a giant puppy pile, and best of all, our parents snuggled with us.

The next morning, after the cows fed us again, Mom and Dad told us we were going to a village called Dinsford.

"I know a Labrador there who can help you," said the collie. "His pet is driving a truck to London, and if you hurry, you can get a ride. When you get to Dinsford, he will be waiting."

This was very good news, and we set out in high spirits. In the bright winter sunshine, scampering along with our parents, it was easy to forget about our troubles.

For a while, anyway.

The black Labrador met us at nightfall and quickly guided us into Dinsford, a quiet village with one street. It was much smaller than London.

He led us through hedges and down a narrow, twisty lane, into an abandoned house with a dirty old fireplace and some broken chairs.

"You'll be safe here," he said, "until Nigel's truck gets fixed." He rubbed a dusty window with his nose so we could see outside. "That's Nigel," he said, pointing to a whiskered man leaning against a truck. "My pet. Isn't he sweet?"

"He looks like he's very nice," said Mom politely.

"Do you know how long we'll have to wait?" asked Dad.

"Shouldn't be long," said the Labrador. "The mechanic's been working on it all day."

The Labrador went outside to pet Nigel, so Mom and Dad kept watch at the window. Meanwhile, Patch challenged me to a race, so we ran from one end of the room to the other while the rest of the puppies cheered us on. I am usually a little faster than Patch (though he is bigger than me), and I won easily, so he challenged me to a wrestling match.

Patch says I cheated when I threw fireplace ashes into his face, but the only rule of dog wrestling is No Biting, which I didn't break, so I called him a Big Sore Loser. So he pushed me into the fireplace, and when I was covered with ashes he called me Little Dirtball. The other pups started laughing and yipping, "Fight! Fight!" and the next thing we knew, Mom and Dad were pulling us apart and scolding us.

Then a very strange thing happened. Right in the middle of telling Patch and me we should be ashamed of ourselves, our parents stopped and looked at each other.

"That's it!" cried Mom. "They can roll in the ashes and hide their spots!"

"Right you are, as usual!" Dad agreed.

And that is how we found out about a new, very dangerous game we were going to play, called Let's Fool Cruella.

8

Nigel

Meanwhile, Cruella and the Bad Men had come to the village looking for us. The sight of them made our parents very anxious. Nigel's truck was repaired and ready to go, waiting just across the street, but Cruella was parked near it.

"I know they're here somewhere," she snapped to the Bad Men.

My parents were afraid we'd never get by her—until they saw me and Patch. Then they realized that we'd stumbled upon the perfect disguise. With ashes covering our spots, we didn't look like Dalmatians!

It was time, they said, to play Let's Fool Cruella.

First, everybody had to roll in the ashes. "Go on, jump in!" cried Dad. "Get as filthy as Patch and Lucky." The puppies were happy to obey, and soon they were all covered with soot.

"Not a spot in sight!" said Mom approvingly. Then Dad told us about the second part of the game: we had to follow the Labrador across the street so he could lift us onto Nigel's truck. "Keep low to the ground, and be as quiet as cats," he said. "Understand?"

We nodded solemnly and Dad lined us up. The Labrador began leading us out, a few at a time. I was in the last group. We ran out into the street, right in front of Cruella's speeding car! She skidded to a stop. We froze in fear. Then we walked slowly and steadily past her. But just as we were about to escape, something really bad happened.

Plop!

"Faster!" Dad whispered anxiously. "The snow's melting! It's washing away the soot on your coats!"

Alarmed, I turned to look at Patch. His disguise was half gone! Behind him, Penny was almost completely white. So was Rolly.

"Oh, no! Our spots are showing!" he whimpered.

I felt like whimpering, too: Cruella was staring straight at us. "Jasper! Horace!" she screeched.

We're done for! I thought. But I had forgotten about Nigel.

We all knew Nigel was good-natured. But we didn't know that when he got behind the wheel he changed: he became a bellowing beast, exploding down the road like a bull with a wasp in its ear.

Just as the last of us climbed into the truck, Nigel took off with a roar. Cruella zoomed after us, honking her horn and shouting.

Nigel just went faster. Cruella tried to push him off the road, but that didn't work, either: he pushed back. And when Cruella made the mistake of driving too close behind him, he slowed down just long enough to hook her car on to his fender.

That did not make her happy. For a few moments Cruella whipped along behind us, powerless to do anything but scream. Some of the puppies were scared, but I growled at her.

Then Horace and Jasper came barreling down a side road. I think they wanted to cut Nigel off, but instead they crashed into Cruella. Sparks and car parts flew as they all landed in a snowy ditch. Cruella called the Bad Men two more names: Idiot and Imbecile. But her angry shouting faded quickly as Nigel sped toward London.

9

Our Pets

We had to bark and bark before Nanny opened the door of the den, and when we streamed in we kept barking, because it was so good to see our pets, not to mention our very own house with its cushions and biscuits and squeaky toys and TV.

When we finally quieted down, Nanny dusted off our sooty coats until we looked like Dalmatians again, which took a long time because there were so many of us. She and Roger and Anita gave us many more hugs, and while they hugged us they counted us.

That took a long time, too. "A hundred and one Dalmatians!" cried Roger, scratching his head. "I can't believe it!"

"I can't, either," said Anita. "What will we do with them all?"

"We'll keep them, of course. We'll get a big place in the country with lots of room for everybody!" That was just what we had hoped he would say, so all one hundred and one of us wagged our tails and did a Happy Wiggle while Anita and Nanny hugged Roger. He really is a fine pet.

He found us a perfect new den, with lots of grass and trees, some cows, and a cat that's a cousin of Tibs. We're even within barking distance of the Colonel and the Labrador; they send us the news sometimes. That's how we heard Cruella was locked up in a big cage as punishment for stealing us. We all yipped with relief.

"We're safe from her at last!" said my parents.

"And we're all together!" I thought, feeling very lucky, indeed.

My story couldn't have a much better ending, could it?

MY SIDE
of the Story

By **Cruella**

As told to Daphne Skinner

Illustrated by the Disney Storybook Artists

1

I, Cruella

I don't understand people these days, I really don't. Either they're getting hard of hearing or unbelievably stupid, or both. If they would only listen properly—or stop being such nitwits—they would never, ever believe the ridiculous accusations that have been flung at me.

I am referring, of course, to the criminal charges against me. What utter nonsense! I, Cruella De Vil, did not kidnap ninety-nine Dalmatian puppies because I wanted their skins! I told the court over and over again that I never intended to harm those puppies, but did they believe me? No! Now, here I sit, in a dreary little jail cell, being punished for a crime I absolutely did not commit.

Justice must be done.

That is why after many weeks of boredom, terrible food, and no satin sheets, I have decided to clear my name. I, Cruella De Vil, am innocent. And I can prove it—by telling my side of the story.

Many people testified against me at my trial. Anita was one of the first, so I'll start with her. I've known Anita since we were schoolgirls, and the poor thing has never had an ounce of sense. The only reason she got good grades was because she studied so hard. If she'd cheated a little on her exams, or paid a scholarship student to do her homework for her, the way I did, she would have had a lot more fun. But, no. She wouldn't even play hooky with me—she was afraid of getting into trouble!

"Just do what I do," I advised. "Whenever the headmistress scolds me I say, 'Daddy might forget to send in one of his big donation checks if you keep hurting my feelings.' It works every time."

My excellent advice fell on deaf ears—as I mentioned, Anita never had much sense. And she proved it a few years later by falling in love with Roger, a penniless songwriter. Then she married him! I told her not to a dozen times, but nothing I said would change her mind. That's Anita for you.

And sure enough, she and Roger ended up in a house the size of a shoe box, living like paupers.

I dreaded speaking with her because her news was always so depressing: "Roger hasn't sold a single song yet," or "I'm doing a little secretarial work to help make ends meet." It always took me a while to recover from our conversations. Going on a shopping spree usually helped.

Then one day Anita mentioned that her dog Perdy was going to have puppies, which was good news for once. Actually, I was thrilled—Perdy is a Dalmatian, and I absolutely adore the breed. Their spotted coats are so striking! And so soft! If anything looks—or feels—nicer than a sleek, polka-dotted Dalmatian puppy, I'd like to know what it is.

Naturally, I wanted to see them right away, but Anita told me I'd have to wait. The puppies weren't due for at least three weeks. Three whole weeks! I can hardly wait an hour for a manicure! You can't imagine what an ordeal this was for me.

Still, I endured. And finally—finally!—Puppy Day arrived.

2

My Inner Voice

Anita and Roger live in a tiny house in a shabby neighborhood. Shockingly, they get by with only one crotchety old servant, who is no help to them at all. Nanny! Her name should be Ninny. They really should replace her, and I said so when I walked in, but Anita simply smiled. Her hearing is failing. I'm sure of it.

At any rate, I forgot about her crabby old Nanny the moment I saw a puppy.

"I'll take it," I cried, pulling out my checkbook and waving it in Anita's face. "I'll take them all!" I began writing a rather large check, thinking Anita and Roger would be grateful. But, no. Before I could sign my name, they stopped me.

"We want to keep them," said Anita.

"We're not selling them," said Roger.

I was dumbfounded. But I didn't try to bully them, as Anita told the court. I simply pointed out the truth.

"This awful little house is much too small for so many puppies," I said. "And you can't possibly have enough money to take care of them. Why the devil do you want to raise them in filth and squalor?"

They didn't even try to answer—they just stood there staring as if I'd coughed up a hairball. Roger's jaw was actually hanging open. It occurred to me that he might be getting hard of hearing, too, so I spoke very loudly and clearly from that point on. I wasn't screaming, as Anita said, I was just making sure they heard me.

"These puppies deserve a good home and I'm offering one," I said. "My home is big enough for a hundred puppies!" My ancestral home was ten times the size of their house, and they knew it, but did that sway them? No.

They turned me away. Every fiber of my being protested when I was forced to leave those poor puppies behind (though I absolutely did not slam the door so hard the glass broke—that's another lie).

I was troubled, though. I tossed and turned all night, while undernourished little Dalmatians cried out to me in my dreams. "Help us, Cruella, help us!" they whimpered. "We need you!"

When I woke, a quiet yet firm inner voice told me exactly what to do: "Cruella," it said, "save those puppies!"

Does it surprise you that I, Cruella De Vil, have an inner voice that prompts me to do good deeds? Or that I am a devoted friend of all creatures great and small, especially Dalmatian puppies? Well, sit down, reader, because I have another surprise for you: long before my visit to Roger and Anita, I'd already rescued dozens of little Dalmatians—from pet shops, breeders, and many undeserving private households. With the help of my assistants, Jasper and Horace (who were still faithful employees then, not the miserable, lying wretches they later became), I had long been whisking puppies away to my house under the cover of darkness. The old family mansion fairly rang with the sound of their merry yipping.

It was music to my ears.

3

Jasper

I thought of going back to Roger and Anita, I really did. Shouldn't I make one more attempt to buy the puppies and give them the home they deserved? I wondered and fretted—until that same quiet inner voice told me it would be a waste of time. "They'll never listen to you, Cruella," it said, and I said, "You're right."

So I sent Jasper and Horace to fetch Perdy's litter. They collected the puppies that night, after explaining to Nanny why it was necessary. Her claim that they locked her in the attic is completely untrue; she did it herself and was too embarrassed to admit it. As I said, the woman's a ninny.

At any rate, all fifteen puppies were soon safely ensconced in my mansion.

I was so relieved to hear it! It warmed my heart to picture them exploring their spacious new home—it is quite grand—and making friends with all the other little Dalmatians in residence. What fun they'd have!

"You've done the right thing, Cruella," said my inner voice, and I had to agree.

But did the jury agree? No! They found me guilty of terrible wrongdoing! Why? I wondered. Why? Day after day, I paced back and forth in my cell, asking myself that question, until I wore holes in my best ostrich-feather slippers.

Finally the answer came to me. "Cruella," said that quiet inner voice I was coming to know so well, "face it. They all lied."

Not even Jasper—who was once a loyal employee—told the truth.

It still pains me to think of how that idiot betrayed me. I'll admit we've had our differences—I did once, quite accidentally, knock him down the stairs when he made me lose my temper—but after that, we got along quite well. So, I was deeply shocked by the hostile things he said about me.

He actually claimed that I cheated him and his partner Horace, which is ridiculous. I was going to pay them for their work, but I was arrested first!

Then he said that I flew into a rage and attacked him while we were discussing the puppies. Nonsense! How could that fool mistake a hearty clap on the back for an assault? It was an employer's love tap, that's all. I never meant to dislocate his shoulder!

But his biggest lie was about my intentions. He called them cruel.

"She meant to murder those dogs," he told the jury. "She wanted to make them into a puppy coat."

Well! I could hardly make myself heard over the explosion of outrage in the courtroom. I tried, believe me, but nobody would listen. They were all shouting, "Shame! Shame!" and "Puppy Monster!" Somebody even pelted me with liver treats.

The truth got lost that day, but it won't be lost forever. For I, Cruella De Vil, was completely misunderstood: I didn't want a puppy *coat*, I wanted a puppy *boat*.

4

The Proud De Vils

Let me explain. The De Vils have always been a seafaring family; our history is long and proud. My great-grandfather, Rathful De Vil, squelched the notorious Banana Mutiny of 1882 (his crew objected to being paid in fruit) with the help of a few eager sharks. My grandfather, Infernal De Vil, imported scores of exotic birds and animals on his ship *The Looter* before a bad-tempered orangutan did him in. My uncle, Coup De Vil, did not go to sea but found great success in America designing large, boatlike cars adorned with fins.

And my mother, Dementia De Vil (who never recovered from the failure of her brilliant invention, the self-inflating bathing suit), claimed that she'd been a narwhal in a previous life.

You could say that the sea was in my blood.

So, launching a puppy boat made perfect sense to me. In my opinion, a combination petting zoo and cruise line was a stroke of genius! I'd call it the S.S. *Spots on the Sea*; the puppies would wear little sailor caps; and customers could enjoy the whole experience in perfect safety (despite any sudden rough weather) because self-inflating bathing suits would be readily available for purchase.

I loved the idea, and I thought the court would, too. Instead, they laughed and jeered. More than one imbecile shouted that I was a liar. I was so hurt.

Then Horace took the stand.

Horace has worked for me for years. He's a fool and he has the grooming habits of a chimpanzee, but I've always treated him well. So I thought he'd show me some loyalty. But no! He testified against me, too, just like Jasper.

His testimony was every bit as damaging.

Take his description of the night I visited my home, after Anita and Roger's puppies had moved in. I'd driven all the way from London, longing to pet as many soft little Dalmatians as I could. I simply couldn't wait to gather the silky things around me like a shawl, so I hurried into the sitting room, where I found Horace half-asleep in front of the television.

"Loafer!" I cried playfully, making him jump. Then—just as a joke, mind you—I poked him with an iron poker before making my request. And he misunderstood me completely! I didn't tell him to *kill* the puppies, I told him to *call* the puppies!

"Call them!" I said. "Call them!"

Perhaps Horace was in such a stupor that he couldn't make sense of my words. Perhaps he was going deaf, like everybody else.

I don't know.

But I do know this: his distorted account of that fateful night helped to put me behind bars. And as long as I'm in jail, the world will just have to get along without a puppy boat!

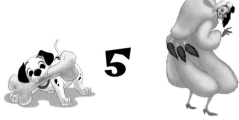

5

The So-Called Truck Driver

And now we come to the saddest part of my tale, the part that makes me weep bitter tears in my cramped, uncarpeted little cell every time I think of it. I'm referring, of course, to my search for the puppies after they blundered out of my home. They got lost somewhere in the snowbound countryside, and I was desperate to find them.

What if they starved or froze to death? What if they damaged their beautiful coats? It was too awful to contemplate. And it was torture to look for the puppies with those morons Horace and Jasper. They drove around witlessly for hours, finding nothing but reasons to complain. Great-grandfather Rathful would have had them keelhauled! As Horace and Jasper had allowed the puppies to get away, I told them—very sweetly, of course—that they wouldn't get a penny until every single one of those Dalmatians was back safe inside.

But did they find them? No!

It was I, Cruella De Vil, who saw paw prints in the snow and tracked the puppies to Dinsford. And it was I, Cruella De Vil, who realized that the poor things were being kidnapped by a devious criminal disguised as a truck driver.

How I wish I could say that it was I, Cruella De Vil, who rescued them from that man! But I did not—and that is my tragedy. Knowing how close I came, and that I failed, feels as bad as a scratchy cashmere sweater, and worse than a torn cuticle.

If only I'd been able to stop that truck! If only Horace and Jasper hadn't crashed into me at exactly the wrong moment! When we all flew into a ditch, the truck got away. And now the worst has happened: the puppies are back with Roger and Anita, who will never, ever give them the loving care that they deserve.

I, Cruella De Vil, am the only one who can do that. Yet I am in prison for six years—unless I get time off for good behavior, whatever that is.

6
Dog Devil

My quiet inner voice has become a little louder these days, though I can't say I mind. I find it comforting.

"Cruella, you did your best," it often tells me. "People may hate you now, but that will change. One day they'll understand your true worth—just give them time."

"But, Inner Voice," I reply, "when will the newspapers stop calling me 'Dog Devil'? When will I stop getting mean letters? When will the world admit that I was right, and everybody else was wrong? I'm so tired of waiting! And by the way, when are they going to let me have some servants in here?"

My inner voice cannot always answer so many questions. When it goes silent, I try not to panic. Instead, I think about good things, like finishing my prison sentence. I'll be getting out in just 275 weeks!

When I'm released, my driver will be waiting. I'll hop in and drive straight to London. And then I'll buy new clothes, lots of them.

For some strange reason, I kind of have a thing for stripes!

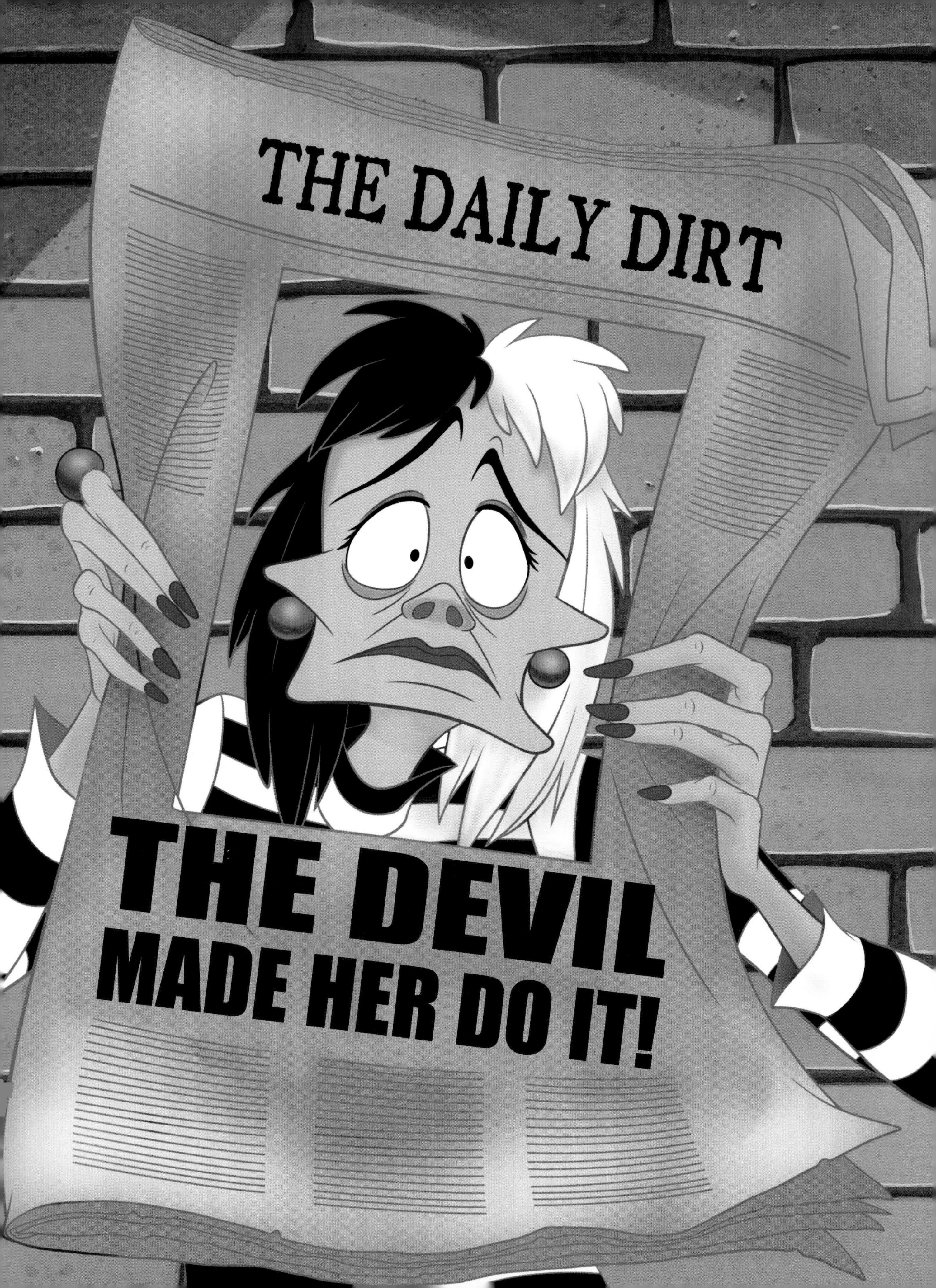
THE DAILY DIRT
THE DEVIL
MADE HER DO IT!